CATWOMAN:

HER ~ SISTER'S ~ KEEPER

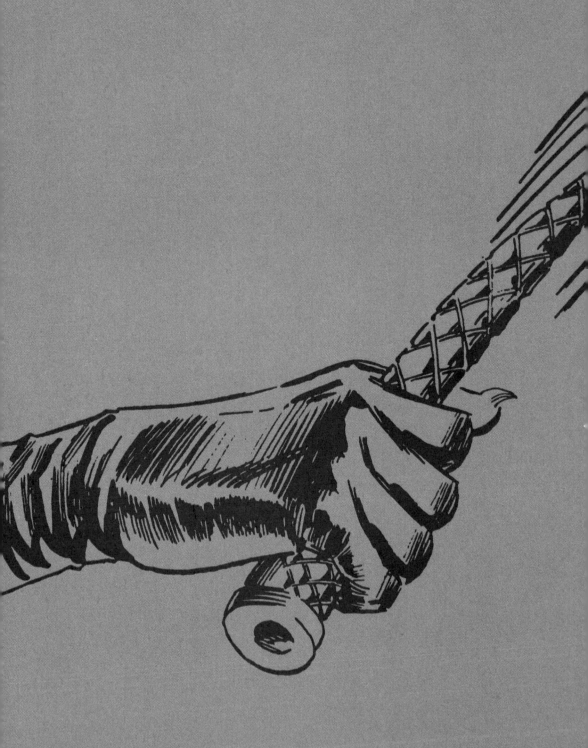

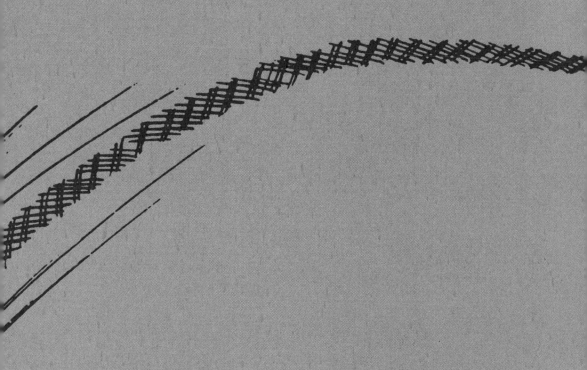

CATWOMAN:

HER ~ SISTER'S ~ KEEPER

MINDY NEWELL ▼ **J.J. BIRCH** ▼ **MICHAEL BAIR**
Writer   Penciller   Inker

AGUSTIN MAS ▼ **ADRIENNE ROY**
Letterer   Colorist

Batman created by **BOB KANE**

CATWOMAN: HER SISTER'S KEEPER

Cover and compilation © 1991 DC Comics Inc. All rights reserved.

Previously published in single magazine issues as CATWOMAN #1-4.
Copyright © 1989 DC Comics Inc.

Batman, Catwoman, and all related characters and indicia
are trademarks of DC Comics Inc.

The stories, characters, and incidents featured in this
publication are entirely fictional.

ISBN: 0-930289-97-8

Published by DC Comics Inc.,
1325 Avenue of the Americas, New York, NY 10019
A Warner Bros. Inc. Company ⓦ
Printed in Canada. First Printing.

Cover Illustration by Brian Stelfreeze
Publication Design by Robbin Brosterman

INTRODUCTION

BY ARCHIE GOODWIN

Something scared me very much when I was five years old. It was a movie, *Cat People*, the first in what would become a series of minor classics in the horror film genre from RKO producer Val Lewton. This 1942 movie, brilliantly and moodily directed by Jacques Tourneur, tells the story of a woman who believes she is descended from an ancient race of shape-changers and that when sensually aroused she will turn into a black panther. A cat-woman.

This volume, which collects the original four-issue *Catwoman* miniseries, is not part of the horror genre, but in reviewing the material to write this introduction, I found myself recalling the film, which I haven't seen or thought about in years. No great surprise. There are definite parallels.

Some are obviously in writer Mindy Newell's cinematic pacing of her terse and nearly caption-less script and the *film noir* look (which Lewton's movies helped create) evoked by the shadowed compositions and page and panel designs in J.J.

Birch and Michael Bair's artwork. But the most striking for me is in the duality of the central character, the use of the cat-form as the only way the heroine can express conflicting aspects of her personality. And—yes, Doctor Freud—her sexuality.

Research indicates that *Cat People* producer Val Lewton and his scriptwriter, DeWitt Bodeen, were inspired to their storyline by a series of fashion designs which featured drawings of women with the heads of cats (RKO gave them the title, ordering Lewton to provide a horror movie to go with it). But the motif of a woman taking on the mantle of a cat to play out forbidden yearnings makes me wonder if it was possible that someone connected with the film saw Catwoman's appearances in *Batman* or *Detective Comics*.

Those appearances began in the spring of 1940 with the first issue of *Batman*. Catwoman was a thrill-seeking jewel thief. She went through a number of alternate identities before being definitely established as Selina Kyle, but wasted no time at all developing into the "good" bad woman with a fatal

attraction for the hero who can bring her downfall. Within the boundaries and limitations of comic books of the period, it was a strong——and mutual——attraction. Over the next forty-plus years, it would hold through many permutations, including several retirements from crime for Selina (during which she was the owner of a pet shop), at least one marriage to Bruce Wayne (an alternate reality was involved), and a high quota of jealousy, betrayal, and down-to-the-wire soul-searching.

Still, while a forties movie like *Cat People* could establish a character's duality of nature and sense of sexual attraction/repulsion as sub-text and psychological underpinning, that was probably never a conscious intention in comics of the day. Some undercurrents can be read into the material from a modern perspective (obviously I'm doing it), but that's all it was. Undercurrents. The aim was for straightforward, exciting stories for a broad, principally young audience.

And that aim didn't change until the audiences began to.

The super-hero and costumed adventurer genre that first made comic books distinct and popular went into decline after World War II and by the fifties had been elbowed aside by a succession of different trends such as western, romance, crime, and horror comics. The archetypes of the genre like *Batman* did not disappear, but they were seriously overshadowed and had to go through some strange maneuvers in order to survive. For Batman and partner, Robin, trips to outer space weren't unknown, and battles with alien monsters became almost as routine as strapping on a utility belt.

In the mid-sixties, there was a super-hero revival with a new emphasis on character and character touches to make the larger-than-life fantasy figures more believable. It worked. It worked well enough that while in the past it was traditional that audiences for comics turned over every three to five years, more of them began staying with the ongoing adventures of their favorite characters. There were always some older readers of comics (this is being written by one of them) but in the past twenty-five years their number has gradually increased——increased to the point that material could be pitched to them directly and to the point that creators and publishers could let the work and

the characters reflect a changing world, attitudes, and concerns.

In the eighties, this culminated in several successful, groundbreaking comics projects. One of the best was *The Dark Knight Returns* by Frank Miller with Klaus Janson and Lynn Varley, published by DC Comics in 1986. It showed a tormented and obsessed Batman in his twilight and gave comics readers (and creators) a new look at how far and how deep the super-hero fantasy concept might be pushed. Questions about the genre were being raised, leading to a reexamination of its characters right down to their roots.

Having explored the end of the Dark Knight's career, Frank Miller next turned to *Batman: Year One*, this time in collaboration with David Mazzucchelli and Richmond Lewis. Respectful of the basics in the Batman legend, *Year One* still manages to fill in many things unaccounted for and unexamined over the years. It does this sometimes disturbingly, but always in a way emotionally true and psychologically valid for the kind of world in which a Batman might reasonably exist today. In particular, James Gordon (before his rise to Commissioner) is

turned from convenient prop into a remarkably complex and fully-fleshed individual, almost upstaging the title character. Less completely developed, but still intriguingly sketched into the storyline, is the woman known as Selina Kyle.

The sketch is broad and, for long-time followers of the Batman mythos, perhaps shocking. Selina Kyle is no pet shop owner in this Gotham City. She is a prostitute, seemingly specializing in domination. She has associations with another young prostitute, Holly, and a pimp called Stan. The emergence of the Batman character becomes a source for drawing her from this life into a new one. That of a jewel thief. The Catwoman.

Sordid. But sensible in the newly established reality, itself a not very exaggerated reflection of what we know about the corruptions of our own world. All broadly sketched. All fairly crying out to be looked at in greater detail—which is what has been done in this collection.

From the hints and incidents of *Batman: Year One*, several of which are reenacted in the pages that follow, Mindy Newell, J.J. Birch, and Michael Bair, working with editors Dennis O'Neil and Dan

Raspler, have woven some intriguing possibilities in answer to the perhaps outraged questions that this new Selina Kyle raises. Some of them, I suspect, tap into the things that scared me when I was five years old and saw the movie *Cat People*.

On the surface, of course, it obviously doesn't take much to scare a five-year-old. Just knowing that I was being taken to a scary movie probably got the ball rolling quite well. The music and sound effects alone could have done the rest. But far more than that stayed with me. Scenes and feelings have taken residence in some far corner of my mind for almost half a century. And reading the material in this book seemed to bring them out again.

I suspect what really scared me about *Cat People* and what I think *Catwoman* also brings to mind is that we identify with the struggle going on in the main character. Consciously or—when I was that five-year-old—unconsciously, we feel there's this dark thing in all of us struggling to get out. Maybe it's anger. Maybe it's sex. Maybe it's *all* the frustrations of being who we are instead of who we'd like to be or feel others want us to be. Whether we're five or whether we're fifty.

It's an old struggle. In 1942, Val Lewton and his collaborators could—within the somewhat unlikely arena of what was supposed to be a cheap horror film—deal with it in an imaginative, perceptive, and surprisingly intense way. In the same period, Batman creator Bob Kane and collaborators such as Bill Finger, Jerry Robinson, and others could not. It was a way of dealing with things that comics—still expanding on their basics—weren't yet suited to try.

It is a tribute to those early comics professionals that, whatever the limitations on them, their creations were still imbued with the rich potential and flexibility to endure, grow, and change for changing times and readerships. Lesser creations would have self-destructed under the demands.

Today comics finally have the same flexibility their best characters possess. Mindy Newell, J.J. Birch, and Michael Bair are able to take the Catwoman character into areas where filmmaker Val Lewton could not have brought his Cat People. They have not constructed a horror story, yet horror is definitely present. In urban violence we may sometimes fear. In psychological violence we may sometimes perpetrate. On each other. And ourselves.

> **"** THAT THE SAINTS MAY ENJOY THEIR BEATITUDE AND THE GRACE OF GOD MORE ABUNDANTLY, THEY ARE PERMITTED TO SEE THE PUNISHMENT OF THE DAMNED IN HELL. **"**
>
> —ST. THOMAS AQUINAS

part *1*

METAMORPHOSIS

DEPT. OF
SANITATION

②

WHEEEEEEEE EEEEEEEEEEEEEEE

PUT THAT THING *DOWN*, SISTER MAGDALENE, AND COME INSIDE.

IT'S *FREEZING* OUT HERE.

YOU'RE NOT BRINGING THAT CREATURE INSIDE... PROBABLY HAS *FLEAS*, AND GOD *KNOWS* WHAT *ELSE!*

YOU SHOULD WATCH YOUR *LANGUAGE*, SISTER ELIZABETH.

I CAN'T HELP IT. NEVER *COULD* STAND CATS.

WE ALWAYS HAD CATS AT HOME.

YOU'VE HEARD NOTHING?

NOTHING.

I'M SORRY, SISTER.

BUT YOU MUSTN'T LOSE FAITH. SIX MONTHS IS NOT SO LONG IN GOD'S PLAN.

IN THIS CITY, IT'S A LIFETIME.

4

SELINA
KYLE?

FLANNERY, GOTHAM VICE.
UP TO TALKING?

5

You'll wear your *KNEES* out praying so much, Sister Magdalene.

Sometimes, Sister Elizabeth, I think you forget we are nuns.

I don't forget, but my eyes aren't blinded by this habit.

I know you're praying for your sister, Magdalene, and I understand, but meanwhile the world is turning, and there are other runaways to help.

And they are here *NOW*.

Forgive me, Sister, I know this is a sin, but--

I think you are a cold and cruel woman.

What I *AM*, Magdalene, is a *REALIST*--

--but we *ALL* have our crosses to bear. OWWW!

ME-OWWWW!

Wretched creature scratched me.

What--?

Well, it's *FREEZING* out there, isn't it?

Here--

8

HOLLY
SAID--

WHAS?

WHAS
THAT?

NOTHING.

WELL, GET
RID OF IT
AND *C'MERE.*

WHAS WITH THE
COAT? COLD?

I GUESS.

SORRY ABOUT
THE OTHER
NIGHT.

NOT
GONNA HOLD
IT 'GAINST ME?

WHERE
ARE THE
CATS?

STAN--THE
CLOSET?

RELAX, SUGAR,
THEYS FINE.
THEYS GET TO ME,
THAS ALL.

I PUT THEM IN THE EMPTY
'PARTNET NEXT DOOR FOR
NOW. THAS ALL.

THIS IS FOR
YOU.

A *CAT*
COSTUME, STAN?
GIVE ME A
BREAK.

HEY BABY, I MAY
HATES THE THINGS,
BUT *BUSINESS* IS
BUSINESS.

PUT IT
ON.

NO. IT'S
DISGUSTING.

DISGUSTIN? HEY
BABY, *YOU* THE ONE
LOVES CATS.

NO SUSHI BAR, TED?

I HATE RAW FISH.

HOW MANY OTHER GIRLS HAS FLANNERY SENT YOU?

WHO?

THE COP WHO GAVE ME YOUR NUMBER.

I DON'T KNOW ANY COP NAMED FLANNERY.

RIGHT. SORRY. YOU'LL TEACH ME *EVERY* THING?

FOR A HUNDRED BUCKS AN HOUR, I WILL.

I DON'T *HAVE* THAT KIND OF MONEY.

NOT MANY DO.

RELAX, SWEETHEART. MAYBE YOU QUALIFY FOR A DISCOUNT.

IF YOU'RE SERIOUS.

1

AAAA

COME ON YOU GUYS--I GOT HIM--

OWWWWW

DAMN IT--

15

NOBODY HURTS HOLLY--

HURTS. BET HE BROKE MY WRIST--

HISSSSSS

EEEEEEEEE

EEEEEEESKREEEECCHH

SELINA GET UP-- SELINA--

FREEZE--

16

YOU'RE LATE.

THERE WAS SOME TROUBLE.

YOU OKAY?

CAN YOU SHOW ME HOW TO USE THIS?

NICE *TOY*. WHERE'D YOU GET IT?

IT WAS A PRESENT.

FOR THE WHORE WHO HAS EVERYTHING.

I FEEL SORRY FOR YOUR BOYFRIEND.

DON'T.

AND I FEEL SORRY FOR YOU.

I BET YOU WERE A SWEET KID ONCE, WITH PIGTAILS AND A GUMBALL OR TWO IN THE BACKPOCKET OF YOUR OVERALLS.

BET YOU WANTED TO BE A *NURSE* OR A *TEACHER*.

SHUT UP.

WHO YOU *REALLY* LASHING OUT AGAINST, SELINA? IT'S NOT THAT PIMP DOWNTOWN.

IF YOU DON'T KNOW HOW TO USE THAT THING, TED, JUST SAY SO. I'LL FIND SOMEBODY ELSE.

NO NEED.

CRAACK

I'M BEING *SERIOUS*, SELINA. THINGS ARE BLOWING *UP* OVER BY ROBINSON *PARK.*

MAYBE *BRANDEN'S* CORNERED A *JAYWALKER.*

TURN THE TV ON, HOLLY. GOT TO HAVE SOMETHING ON THIS...

...REPORT THAT THE *BATMAN* HAS BEEN SURROUNDED BY GOTHAM POLICE AFTER HE ATTACKED TWO OFFICERS-- ONE OF THEM HERO COP LIEUTENANT JAMES GORDON--

SELINA-- IT'S *BATMAN*-- CAN WE--

--THE VIGILANTE IS NOW TRYING TO *HIDE* IN AN ABANDONED TENEMENT OFF ROBINSON PARK--GUNFIRE HAS BEEN HEARD-- AND EXPLOSIONS--

WHAT THE HELL. GRAB YOUR COAT.

DOWN, OTTO. THERE'S *PLENTY.*

--NOW THERE IS TENSE *SILENCE*-- EYEWITNESSES SAY A HEAVILY ARMED *SWAT* TEAM OF EIGHTEEN MEN HAS ENTERED THE BUILDING--

--STAND *BACK*-- LET US DO OUR *JOB*--

-- BATMAN, SELINA-- SOMEBODY JUST SAID HE'S *ALIVE*--

--MAYBE WE'LL *SEE* HIM--

WE'LL SEE HIS *CORPSE,* HOLLY...

19

NO MORE. NOT TODAY. I CAN'T DO IT.

YES YOU CAN.

I'M TIRED, I'M DIZZY, I DON'T FEEL GOOD, LEAVE ME *ALONE!*

GET UP AND STOP WHINING.

I'M *NOT* WHINING, I'LL DO IT *TOMORROW.*

TOMORROW? TOMORROW'S FOR *TOPEKA.* THIS AIN'T TOPEKA, SELINA.

THIS IS *REAL,* THIS IS *LIFE,* THIS IS *GOTHAM CITY...*

...AND IT EATS WHINERS FOR *APPETIZERS.* IT'S *ALREADY* HAD A *TASTE* OF YOU. HOW MUCH *MORE* DO YOU WANT TO GIVE IT?

TED, YOU'RE *HURTING* ME.

GOOD.

LET *GO.*

BREAK *FREE.*

I *CAN'T.*

YOU'RE NOT EVEN *TRYING.*

I'LL *HURT* YOU.

THAT'S THE *IDEA.*

STOP IT.

STOP IT, YOU'RE HURTING ME --

OTTO, GET *OFF* THAT!

STUPID CAT. RUIN EVERYTHING.

RUIN *WHAT*?

NOTHING.

SELINA-- RUIN *WHAAT*?

WE GOT ANY THREAD AROUND HERE, HOLLY?

LOOK AT THIS. CLAWED A HOLE RIGHT *THROUGH* IT.

NO-- *I* THINK IT'S *WEIRD*-- STAN GIVING YOU THAT THING-- HE *HATES CATS*--

YEAH--

--THAT'S HIS *PROBLEM*.

"STAN--"

"WAS THE MATTER? WHERE ARE YOU?"

"IN A PHONE BOOTH. HE WAS WIRED, STAN, STRUNG OUT-- PULLED A KNIFE--GOD, I THINK HE'S DEAD, I KNOW HE'S DEAD. WHAT'LL WE DO?"

"ANYBODY SEE? CORS?"

"NO. NO, I DON'T THINK SO. GOD, STAN, I'M SCARED."

"OKAY, JUS' STAY COOL, THAS RIGHT, I'M COMIN'. BE AT THE REGULAR SPOT."

"BUT WHAT IF--"

"DON' TALK TO NOBODY, DON' DO NOTHIN...

"...JUS WAITS TIL YOU SEE ME."

TO BE CONTINUED...

" WE BE OF ONE BLOOD, THOU AND I. "

—RUDYARD KIPLING

part **2**

DOWNTOWN BABYLON

YOU *CUT* ME, WOMAN, YOU *CRAZY?*

NOW I GOTS TO *TEACH* YOU A LESSON *AGAIN.*

TEACH ME A LESSON, STAN. *AGAIN.*

3

AND THEN SHE RAN AWAY. I *STARTED* TO RUN AFTER HER, BUT THERE WAS THAT *MAN*--

YOU MEAN *PIMP!*

AND HE WAS *HURT!*

YOU'RE A BETTER NUN THAN I AM, GUNGA DIN.

SISTERS, *PLEASE*-- OKAY, JUST FOR THE HELL OF IT--EXCUSE *ME* SISTERS--

LET'S SAY THIS GIRL *IS* SISTER MAGDALENE'S SISTER.

WHY'D SHE RUN *AWAY* FROM YOU?

SHE'S FRIGHTENED, CONFUSED, EMBARRASSED--

RUNNING HAS *ALWAYS* BEEN HER WAY, DETECTIVE FLANNERY.

WHAT ABOUT THE *COSTUME?*

I--DON'T KNOW.

CAN *YOU* EXPLAIN IT, DETECTIVE?

I CAN TAKE A *STAB* AT IT --

WE GOT THIS *SCREWBALL* LOOSE HERE, RIGHT? DRESSES UP LIKE A *BAT*, BEATS UP ON THE *LOW*-LIFE, THE WHOLE *ZORRO* NUMBER, *EAST END* VERSION.

NOW IT LOOKS LIKE WE GOT *ANOTHER* ONE. ONLY *THIS* ONE'S A *WOMAN*, AND INTO *CATS*. AND HER SISTER'S A *SISTER* --

OR SO THE *SISTER* SAYS.

YOU DON'T BELIEVE ME, DO YOU?

OH, I BELIEVE THE PART ABOUT THIS *CAT*-WOMAN.

YOU JUST DON'T BELIEVE WE'RE *RELATED*.

'FRAID NOT.

THANK YOU FOR YOUR TIME --

WHAT IS THE PIMP'S *NAME*, PLEASE?

WHAT?

IS HE HERE? I WANT TO TALK TO HIM.

SORRY. LEGALLY COULDN'T HOLD HIM.

I'LL *FIND* HIM. OR HER. I'LL WALK THE *STREETS* 'TIL I *DO*.

A STREETWALKING *NUN*. WHAT A CONCEPT.

I *MEAN* IT.

YOU *DO* AND I'LL *ARREST* YOU FOR *SOLICITING*, SISTER!

STICK TO *PRAYER*. IT'S A *LOT SAFER*.

BUT CHEER UP... MAYBE HE'LL COME TO *BINGO* WEDNESDAY NIGHT.

6

7

8

SELINA, SHE HAD A *PICTURE* OF YOU--

SELINA, ANSWER ME--

WHAT ARE YOU *DOING* IN THERE? SELINA--

YOU'VE BEEN ACTING *REALLY WEIRD*. I MEAN--

WHAT ABOUT STAN--

STAN'S *YESTERDAY'S* GARBAGE.

I DON'T KNOW, SELINA-- I MEAN, YOU SPENT ALL OUR *MONEY* ON THAT COSTUME--

I MEAN, IT'S PRETTY *QUEER*--

I MEAN--

IT'S *MONEY*, HOLLY. BE A KICK. JUST *WATCH*.

SELINA-- WHAT ABOUT THE *NUN*--

9

DAMMIT--

I TOLD YOU TO STAY *OFF* THE STREET, SISTER *MAGDALENE.*

OR YOU'D *ARREST* ME FOR SOLICITING. I REMEMBER.

BOOK ME, *DANNO.* I *SHOULD.*

I CAN JUST *SEE* THE HEADLINES.

ME TOO.

HAVE A NICE DAY, DETECTIVE.

THIS ISN'T *SMART* OF YOU, SISTER. LOTS OF THINGS *HAPPEN* TO WOMEN IN THE EAST END. ALL *KINDS* OF WOMEN.

TOP PRESS

I'M A *NUN,* DETECTIVE.

ALL KINDS.

SO? SO NOTHING.

WHY DON'T WE JUST TAKE...

YOU CAN'T MANHANDLE A NUN, FRANK.

YEAH, YOU'RE RIGHT.

PUBLICITY WILL KILL US IF SHE GETS HURT.

I DUNNO, I FEEL LIKE I'M MISSING SOMETHING--

LIKE WHAT?

I DUNNO THERE'S SOMETHING FAMILIAR ABOUT THAT NUN.

MAYBE YOU BUSTED HER SISTER.

FROM YOUR MOUTH TO GOD'S EARS--

THANKS, FRANK.

WHAT'D I SAY?

MAGGIE--

YOU SURE LOOK *DIFFERENT*. *DAMN* DIFFERENT.

PLEASE DON'T CURSE.

WELL *EXCUSE* ME. I *FORGOT* ABOUT YOUR *VIRGIN* EARS.

I'VE BEEN LOOKING FOR YOU.

I *KNOW*. THE WHOLE *WORLD* KNOWS.

I'LL MAKE US SOME TEA-- I MEAN *COFFEE*, YOU LIKE *COFFEE*, I REMEMBER POP ALWAYS SAID IT WOULD *STUNT* YOUR *GROWTH* AND *LOOK*, YOU'RE *TALLER* THAN *HE* WAS--

I'M *BABBLING*, AREN'T I--

NOW WHAT?

13

NOW WE SAY GOODBYE.

WHAT?

YOU WERE LOOKING FOR ME. HERE I AM. NOW WE SAY GOODBYE. THAT'S THE *LITANY*, ISN'T IT--

OR HAS SOMETHING *NEW* BEEN ADDED?

POP IS DEAD.

WHEN?

TWO MONTHS AGO. HIS HEART GAVE OUT.

STAY OFF THE *STREETS*, MAGGIE. I DON'T NEED *YOU* ON MY CONSCIENCE.

YOU'RE RUNNING *OUT* OF *ESCAPES*--

YOU'RE GOING TO HIT A *DEAD END!*

14

DO YOU *HEAR* ME? I *KNOW* YOU CAN *HEAR* ME--

YOU'RE ACTING LIKE A *CHILD*-- WHEN ARE YOU GOING TO GROW *UP* AND *ACCEPT* LIFE--

INSTEAD OF *FIGHTING* IT? THE WORLD DOESN'T ROTATE AROUND *YOU*, KIDDO. MOM LEFT *US*. POP DIDN'T DIE TO PUNISH *YOU*--

NOBODY HAS IT *IN* FOR *YOU*.

SHE AIN' GONNA LISSEN, SISTER.

SHE GOTS A STUBBUN STREAK, AIN' SHE--

15

C'MON, GEORGE, YOU KNOW THE STORY. PALM *OPEN*, MOUTH--

--*SHUT*. YEAH, YEAH, YOU'RE *REAL* ETHICAL, TEDDY.

WANT A BEER?

THANKS.

PEOPLE COME IN HERE, THEY *SWEAT* A LITTLE, *TALK* A LITTLE--

I'M LIKE THEIR BARTENDER, ONLY *HEALTHIER.*

SO HOW *ETHICAL* YOU *FEELING* TODAY, TEDDY?

WHAT'RE YOU DOING, GEORGE? TRYING TO SET ME UP? YOU WEARING A *WIRE?*

ANYTHING *I* CAN DO, YOU CAN DO *BETTER.*

GEORGE! YOU CUT ME TO THE *QUICK!*

CUT IT *OUT*, TEDDY.

'KAY--SO WHA'D'YA WANT TO KNOW?

SELINA KYLE.

NICE LEGS.

WHAT *ELSE* YOU KNOW ABOUT HER?

LIKE, WHERE IS SHE?

16

ZIRCONS. RHINESTONES. SEMI-PRECIOUS SPARKLERS.

COULD'VE DONE BETTER MYSELF. EVEN WITH GIVING STAN HIS. AND NOT EVEN ONE WORD ON THE TUBE OR THE IN THE PAPERS.

HOW DO I LOOK?

CAN I WEAR THIS OUT TONIGHT?

HAVE TO AIM HIGHER NEXT TIME. GET THEM TO NOTICE.

AND THIS? SELINA--

RREWOW

KNOK KNOK

WHO'S THAT--

MAYBE THIS--

THROW THAT STUFF UNDER THE BED, HOLLY. HURRY UP--

SELLING BINGO CARDS, DETECTIVE FLANNERY?

MAY WE COME IN?

GOT A WARRANT?

THIS ISN'T ABOUT YOU. IT'S ABOUT SISTER MAGDALENE.

WHO?

17

... THEY *GET* LIKE THAT. *HAVE* TO. *JUNGLE* LAW. SURVIVAL OF THE *FITTEST*...

... GOOD EXCUSE AS *ANY.* GOOD A *WAY* AS ANY-- DOWN *HERE.* SO I *HELPED* A LITTLE...

TOUGH LITTLE ALLEY CAT. NOT EVEN *TWENTY.*

SHE *KNEW* YOU.

... SO *WHAT?* I'M NOT THE *ONLY* ONE. YOU GET *TIRED* OF CORPSES IN *TRAINING* BRAS.

SHE GOT BEAT UP BY HER PIMP A FEW MONTHS AGO. I GOT ASSIGNED TO THE CASE. *COMPLETELY* UNCOOPERATIVE-- LIKE *TODAY*...

GIRLSxx

DETECTIVE-- I'M NOT A PRIEST.

YOU THINK I'M *CONFESSING,* SISTER? OKAY. I *CONFESS.* I'M *NEGLIGENT* AND *CYNICAL* AND A *STUBBORN JACKASS* AND A *LAZY COP.* I ADMIT IT. *MEA CULPA*--

I LET IT HAPPEN--

YOU COULDA *TOLD* ME, SELINA--

I *WOULDN'T* 'F TOLD ANYBODY--

SO HOW COME I DON'T FEEL *CLEANSED?*

I LET IT HAPPEN--

YOU *REALLY* HURT MY FEELINGS, SELINA-- *REALLLY*--

I DON'T *BELIEVE* IT! *YOU*--FEEDING THE *CATS*?

SOMEBODY HAS TO-- I CAN'T LET THE WRETCHED CREATURES *STARVE*, CAN I!?

SO MAYBE WE LOADED THE GUN, BUT *SHE* PULLED THE TRIGGER.

SO THAT *ABSOLVES* US OF ANY RESPONSIBILITY?

HEY, BUDDY-BOY, *MARTYRDOM'S* YOUR RELIGION, *NOT* MINE.

I THOUGHT WE WEREN'T GOING TO *DO* THIS ANYMORE, SELINA--

WE'RE NOT.

BUT WE *ARE*--

AREN'T WE? WE'RE WAITING.

FOR *WHAT*?

THE RIGHT CUSTOMER.

WHAT'S THE *DIFFERENCE*-- I'M *HUNGRY* AND I'M *COLD.* I WANNA GO *HOME*--

SELINA--

BINGO--

SELINNAA--

HEY. CANDYMAN....

SELINA--

20

...NICE WHEELS.

HEY, SELINA--GIRL, YOU LOOKING *GOOD*. WHERE YOU *BEEN*?

WHERE YOU BEEN?

HERE AND THERE, HERE AND THERE.

SURE DO LIKE THIS *CAR*.

BET IT *RIDES* GREAT.

REAL LEATHER INSIDE.

IT'S NOT *FAIR*-- I WAITED *WITH YOU*-- SELINA--

I THOUGHT STAN HAD A *THING* ABOUT HIS *WOMEN* AND HIS *FRIENDS*.

I'M NOT *HIS* WOMAN.

ANYMORE. YEAH, I HEARD YOU DUMPED HIM. YOU GOT *GUTS*, LADY.

HE'S NOT SO TOUGH.

HE PUT *YOU* IN THE HOSPITAL.

SCARED HE'LL FIND OUT WE'VE BEEN *TOGETHER*, 'SKEEVERS?

HELL, NO!

GOOD. 'CAUSE HE'S *GOT* SOMETHING OF MINE...

...AND I WANT IT *BACK*.

SCARED TO ASK HIM *YOURSELF*, SELINA?

HELL, NO!

I CAN'T *FIND* HIM, THAT'S ALL. I THOUGHT *YOU'D* KNOW.

Y'ALL BEING SUCH *GOOD* FRIENDS AND ALL--

21

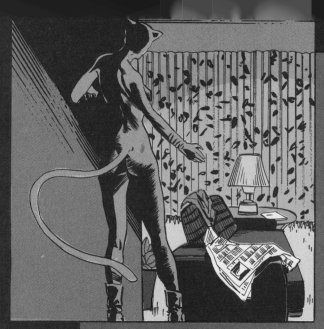

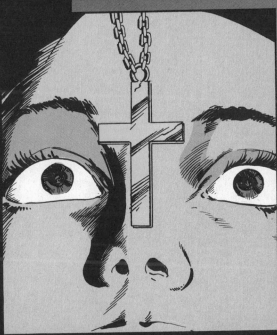

23

"A PERFECTLY NORMAL
PERSON IS RARE IN OUR
CIVILIZATION."

—KAREN HORNEY

part

3

GOTHIC BAPTISM

2

DAMMIT--

SPLASH

WHERE IS HE?

HISSSS

PLEASE-- DON'T HURT ME--

HISSST

OHGODOHGOD- ALLRIGHTALLRIGHTI'LL TELL YOUANYTHING--

TELL ME. THE PIMP CALLED STAN--

4

--THE ONE YOU USED TO WORK FOR--

--TILL COUNCILMAN CROWLY SET YOU UP HERE.

I'MNOTSURE-IMEAN--

THE *SUPPLY DEPOT*, AVENUE F TRAIN. ON EIGH AVENUE. MAYBE THERE, MAYBE *BRUZINSKY'S THEAT* THE OLD STRIP JOINT. O SECOND AND SIXTH.

HSSSS

COUNCILMAN CROWLY HAS GOOD TASTE.

AT LEAST IN JEWELS.

TELL NO ONE I WAS HERE--

AIEEEEE

BUT FROM WHERE--

THEN HE REMEMBERS. THE FIGHT WITH THE PIMP.

皮牛全 回四

THAT'S WHERE HE SAW THE CUFFLINK.

HE CAN ASK QUESTIONS. LEARN THE PIMP'S NAME. LEARN WHERE HE HANGS OUT.

PIMPS AREN'T SUICIDAL. SOMEONE OR SOMETHING PUSHED HIM INTO ABDUCTING THAT NUN.

FIND HIM. AND FIND THE NUN.

HE FINDS HER--HE FINDS ALL THE ANSWERS.

AND GET ALL THE ANSWERS.

7

CLICK

WHAT THE HELL WAS *THAT?* I THOUGHT HE WAS GONNA *DARE* HER TO COME AFTER HIM, AND THEN HE JUST HANGS UP.

DOESN'T MATTER. SHE'LL BE OUT AFTER HIM ANY MINUTE.

BUT SHE DOESN'T KNOW WHERE HE *IS.*

DON'T BET ON IT.

WHERE ARE YOU *GOING--*

OUT--

YOU JUST GOT *IN--*

FEED THE CATS, HOLLY--

NO-- SELINA-- YOU DON'T EVEN KNOW WHERE HE *IS--*

YES I *DO--*

YEAH? *WHERE?*

BRUZINSKY'S THEATRE.

NO TRAIN SOUNDS.

HOW DO YOU KNOW?

A WOMAN IN A TUB TOLD ME.

HUH?

FORGET IT. NOW, GET OUT OF THE WAY--

NO. NOT IN THE *COSTUME--* I HEARD ON THE STREET TONIGHT ABOUT YOU AT *CROWLEY'S* PLACE-- SHE WAS TALKING ALL *OVER* THE PLACE ABOUT THE *LADY CAT--*

WHAT IF STAN'S SETTING YOU *UP?* DON'T MAKE IT *EASY* FOR'IM, SELINA--

TAKE THE COSTUME *OFF. PLEASE.*

NO.
YES.
NO.
NO.
YES.
NO.
NO.

ANYTHING *ELSE* YOU WANT TO KNOW?

ARE YOU GOING TO *HELP* US?

WHAT FOR--

SO YOU DON'T GET *HURT*, KITTEN.

OW--

OR IS THAT THE KIND OF GAMES YOU AND YOUR SICKO FRIENDS ARE INTO--

I DON'T REALLY *CARE* IF YOU AND THE NUN *ARE* SISTERS OR *NOT*, BUT I *DO* CARE ABOUT *CIVILIANS* GETTING IN THE WAY OF *PERSONAL VENDETTAS*--

YEAH, A NICE PRIVATE LITTLE WAR--THAT'S WHAT WE *GOT* HERE, AIN'T IT?-- ONLY IT GOT OUT OF HAND, *DIDN'T* IT, SELINA--

YOU NEVER THOUGHT IT WOULD GET *THIS* PERSONAL, OR *THIS* PRIVATE--

12

DID YOU?

SHE DID IT TO *HERSELF*, RUNNING AROUND, EXPOSING HER-SELF TO CREEPS LIKE STAN--

WHERE'D SHE THINK SHE WAS, *DISNEYLAND*--?

FEELING *GUILTY*, SELINA?

WELL, I DON'T GIVE A *DAMN* IF YOU'RE GUILTY OR NOT--

I WANT THIS THING *FINISHED*. NOW, YOU GOT A *CHOICE*, LADY. HELP *ME*, OR *HANG* WITH *HIM*. AND JUST *REMEMBER*--

YOU OWE *ME*.

FOR *WHAT*--

TED GRANT.

WHO?

YOU KNOW *EXACTLY* WHO. THE GUY WHO TAUGHT YOU TO FIGHT.

THE GUY I SENT YOU TO.

HAVE IT YOUR WAY.

AM I *FREE* TO GO?

WE LET HER GO?

IT'S *HER* FUNERAL.

BUT--

GOT HER, MARK?

HEADING SOUTH DOWN SECOND...

SHE JUST TURNED LEFT ON NASSAU.

ALL RIGHT, ALL UNITS COPY. STAY ALERT, I DON'T WANT TO LOSE HER...

...WEST ON FULTON...

...HEADING DOWNTOWN AGAIN... ON AVENUE A...

JUST WENT INTO A BODEGA ON AVENUE A AND SECOND...

...HAS COME YET

MAYBE WE SHOULD CHECK THIS OUT?

WAIT. LOOK.

HE'S HEADING [B]CK TOWARD... [W]AIT A MINUTE--

THAT LITTLE SLUT--

SHE'S ON TO US. LEADING US IN CIRCLES.

LAUGHING ALL THE WAY.

YEAH. BUT HE WHO LAUGHS LAST--

JOE'S BAR

NO PARKING

WHERE'D SHE GO?

FIRE ESCAPE?

SO FAST?

MUST'VE CLIMBED IN A WINDOW--WHAT'S THAT?

HSSSST

NOTHING. A CAT.

KINDA BIG FOR A CAT.

15

16

MURDERER!

HELP...

...HELP ME...

MAGGIE--?

CRACKKK

:WHOUFF:

BABY DOLL--

YOU GOTS IT ALL WRONG, SUGAR--

:NGGHHH:

20

GOD...HELP US...HELP HER...

YOU BLAMIN ME FOR YOUR SIST'R, THAS WRONG, BABY. YOUR SIST'R, SHE GOT HERSEF IN TROUBLE, I DIDN' GO LOOKIN' FOR HER, SHE COMES TO ME--

CLICK

AN' THEN I TELLS HER--

WHAT, STAN? WHAT'D YOU TELL HER?

I TELLS HER, YOU AN' ME, WE PLAY THIS GAME ALLS THE TIME, GO HOME TO YOUR CONVENT, I SAYS, BUT SHE WANTS TO PLAY TOO--

...PLEASE, GOD, I DON'T WANT TO DIE...

--BUT WE DON'T NEED HER, STAN. YOU DON'T NEED HER--

IT'S ME YOU NEED--IT'S ALWAYS BEEN ME--HASN'T IT--

AND I'M HERE, STAN--ALL OF ME--JUST FOR YOU--

YOU LYIN'! YOU DON' LIKE BEIN' TOUCHED! I KNOWS YOU DON'!

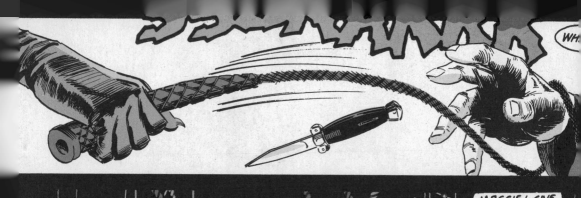

To Be Continued

part 4

CONSECRATION

WAS HOLED UP HERE FOR A WHILE. DRESSING ROOM'S A MESS--LOT OF BEER CANS AND McDONALD'S WRAPPERS IN THERE--

ANY CRUCIFIXES OR ROSARY BEADS?

NO, SIR. AT LEAST NOT YET. THEY'RE STILL DIGGING THROUGH THE GARBAGE

MAYBE HE NEVER *HAD* THE NUN.

OH, HE HAD HER, CAPTAIN STRUNK. I KNOW IT IN MY *GUT*.

WHAT YOU *NEED*, PAL, IS SOLID, HARD EVIDENCE.

I JUST HOPE IT DOESN'T SHOW UP IN *PIECES*, IF YOU GET MY *DRIFT*.

YOU PEOPLE IN HOMICIDE HAVE SUCH *DELICATE* WAYS OF PUTTING THINGS.

HEY! *YOU!* KID! GET OFF MY *CAR!*--

DON'T GET *CRANKY*, GEORGE. I KNOW HOW RELIABLE GUTS ARE. BUT THEY DON'T HOLD UP IN *COURT*.

HEY, YOU *HEAR* ME--?!

MAYBE HE *DID* KILL 'ER, DETECTIVE.

MAYBE--

GET OFF!

LITTLE *PUNK!*

BUT WHO KILLED HIM?

HEY, DETECTIVE, AIN'T THAT--?

6

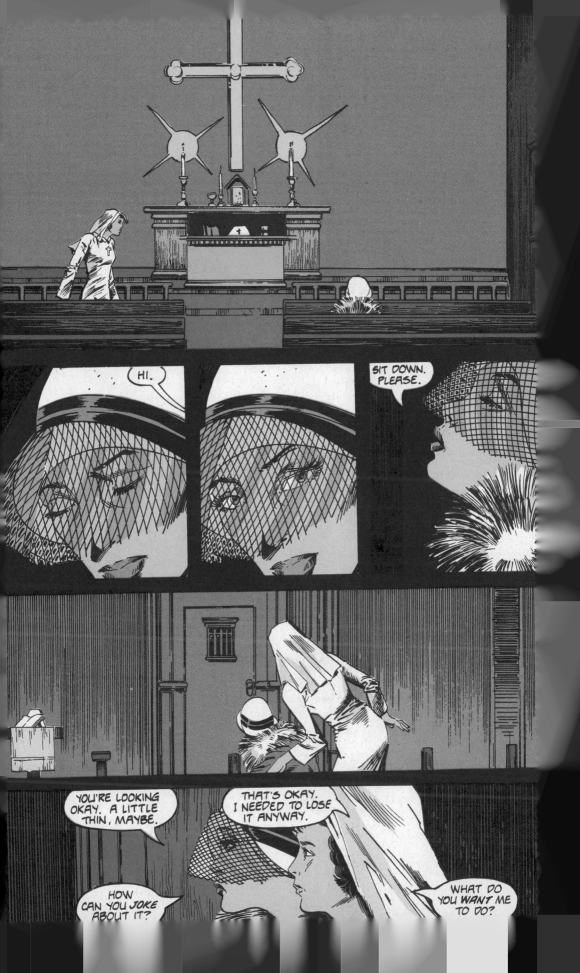

CRY! SCREAM! CURSE ME OUT! TELL ME TO GET OUT AND NEVER COME BACK!

I DID ALL THAT. I CRIED, AND I SCREAMED, AND I'VE HATED AND CURSED YOU, AND THIS GOD-FORSAKEN CITY, AND THIS WHOLE STINKIN' BALL OF WAX WORLD--

I WAS IN THE HOSPITAL FOR THREE WEEKS AND YOU KNOW WHAT I DID BETWEEN CRYING AND SCREAMING AND CURSING YOU?

PRAY FOR FORGIVENESS?

I THOUGHT OF ALL THE DIFFERENT WAYS I COULD KILL MYSELF.

YOU KNOW-- WHAT'S BLACK AND WHITE AND RED ALL OVER...

KIND OF SICK, WASN'T IT? LIKE DEAD BABY JOKES.

STOP IT! THIS ISN'T YOU TALKING! IT'S STAN, AND IT'S ME, AND IT'S THE EAST END AND IT'S EVERY-THING--

BUT IT'S NOT YOU--!

IT'S THIS--!

THIS!!

8

10

DON'T LET THE CAT OUT. LET IT HURT.

WHO DID THIS, HOLLY?

CAPTAIN STRUNK.

STRUNK?? ARE YOU CRAZY?

STRUNK.

UH-UH. NO WAY.

LET ME TELL YOU *ABOUT* CAPTAIN ETHAN STRUNK.

HOLLY'S NOT A LIAR.

SHE'S A WHORE.

YOU TOLD ME ONCE EVEN WHORES GOT RIGHTS. PROVE IT.

TWENTY-SEVEN YEAR VETERAN, GOES TO CHURCH EVERY SUNDAY. NEVER'S TAKEN A PENNY HE DIDN'T EARN. KNOWS THE FAMILIES OF EVERY COP IN HIS DEPARTMENT. NEVER FORGETS BIRTHDAYS, HOLIDAYS, ANNIVERSARIES. PROMOTED A WOMAN TO SECOND-IN-COMMAND AND HAS A BLACK DAUGHTER-IN-LAW.

11

YOU GETTING THE *PICTURE*, MISS KYLE?

THE BASTARD ATTACKED HOLLY.

Y'KNOW, HOLLY WAS AT THE SCENE OF THE CRIME A FEW WEEKS AGO. WHERE WERE *YOU*?

DON'T TRY TO CHANGE THE SUBJECT.

I'M NOT. STAN'S DEAD, THE NUN'S BACK AT THE MISSION, GORDON SAYS EVERYONE SHOULD BE HAPPY. SO I'M HAPPY--

--GOT A LOT OF *UNANSWERED* QUESTIONS, BUT I'M HAPPY.

ANYWAY, HOLLY WAS CLIMBING ALL OVER STRUNK'S CAR TRYING TO *RUBBERNECK*, HE GOT PISSED, GOT A LITTLE *ROUGH* WITH HER--

HEY, LOOK, MAYBE THE KID'S TRYING TO GET *BACK* AT HIM.

AND *JUSTICE* FOR ALL.

14

YOU'RE A WOMAN--?!!

HISSSSSTT!

OKAY, LADY, I DON'T KNOW WHAT THIS IS ABOUT OR WHAT YOU'RE ON--

BUT YOU'LL REGRET EVER SEEING ME.

SWAAK

WWHHAAAK

EEEAARR!AAA!

18

THUNK

THE NUN IS WORRIED ABOUT YOU.

STAY OUT OF THIS.

I CAN'T.

MOVE OUT OF THE WAY.

HE'S SICK.

SO WHAT? THE WHOLE WORLD'S SICK.

MAYBE. BUT NOBODY'LL DEFEND A COP-KILLER. NOBODY.

22

23

The End